ABBE
Regional Library System

W9-BNQ-874

DISCARD

MY
DOG,
MY
HERO

MY DOG, MY HERO

BETSY BYARS
BETSY DUFFEY LAURIE MYERS

ILLUSTRATED BY LOREN LONG

HENRY HOLT AND COMPANY

NEW YORK

Henry Holt and Company, LLC
Publishers since 1866
115 West 18th Street, New York, New York 10011

Henry Holt is a registered trademark of Henry Holt and Company, LLC
Text copyright © 2000 by Betsy Byars, Betsy Duffey, and Laurie Myers
Illustrations copyright © 2000 by Loren Long. All rights reserved.
Published in Canada by Fitzhenry & Whiteside Ltd.,
195 Allstate Parkway, Markham, Ontario L3R 4T8.

Library of Congress Cataloging-in-Publication Data
Byars, Betsy Cromer.
My dog, my hero / by Betsy Byars, Betsy Duffey, Laurie Myers;
illustrated by Loren Long.
p.   cm.
Summary: A panel of three judges has to decide which dog
out of eight finalists deserves to win the title of My Hero.
[1. Dogs—Juvenile fiction. 2. Dogs—Fiction.] I. Duffey, Betsy.
II. Myers, Laurie.   III. Long, Loren, ill.   IV. Title.
PZ10.3.B965Mu   2000   [Fic]—dc21   99-44496

ISBN 0-8050-6327-7 / First Edition—2000
Printed in the United States of America on acid-free paper. ∞

1   3   5   7   9   10   8   6   4   2

To our dogs and yours

—B. B., B. D., AND L. M.

*For Tracy, who lets Stella give kisses
to Griffin and Graham*

—L. L.

DOGS IN ORDER OF APPEARANCE

Smiley 3

Bear 8

Munchkin 16

Old Dog 20

Buster 25

Blue 31

Little Bit 37

Dopey 42

The Daily Chronicle

My Hero to Be Chosen

Eight FINALISTS will compete tonight for the title *My Hero*. The winner will wear the coveted gold My Hero medal. These brave and courageous dogs will each appear with their nominator, who will tell their story. A panel of judges will select the winner. The judges are dog lovers as well as authors: Betsy Byars, Betsy Duffey, and Laurie Myers. The program will be televised by WDOG. Good luck to all the heroes.

Smiley

"**B**ull's out!"

When I heard Daddy yell that I knew I was in trouble.

Smiley and I were out in the north pasture. I was looking for arrowheads, and Smiley was keeping me company. I'd named the dog Smiley because that's what he did. He was the happiest-looking dog I ever saw in my life.

"Smiley," I said, "we better shut that gate."

When we'd come into the pasture the gate had been open, and since there wasn't anything to keep in or out, we'd let it be.

I started for the gate. As soon as Smiley saw

where I was heading, he passed me—he always liked to be in the lead. And then both of us stopped.

The bull was coming through the open gate. He paused to decide who to go for, and then he saw me.

Now, this was a mean bull—we called him Toro because he acted like those bulls you see in bullfights, only those bulls have a reason to be tossing their heads and running at people, because men are sticking them with swords. Toro just acted that way out of meanness.

There was a tree in the middle of the pasture and I turned and ran for that. My only hope was to get to the tree before the bull got to me.

I ran like I'd never run before. I could hear the bull's hoofs pounding the dry pasture behind me. They were getting louder, closer. I wasn't going to make it.

Then I could hear yapping from Smiley, but I didn't look around.

I was running so fast that, when I got to the tree and grabbed a limb, my whole body swung around. I scrambled up on the first limb and then on up the trunk, high as I could get.

I couldn't see what was happening, but I could hear. Smiley was still yapping, and though I couldn't see him, I knew he was nipping at the bull's legs.

I yelled, "I'm all right, Smiley! Run!"

Then I heard a cry of pain—a sound Smiley had never made in his life. Then there was a thud.

I moved out on the limb to where I could peer through the leaves. I could see the bull, looking around for something else to chase. And I could see Smiley lying on his side about twelve feet away.

I thought Smiley was dead, but I kept yelling, "Smiley, Smiley," in case he wasn't.

Smiley didn't move.

I thought he might at least thump his tail to show me he was alive. He didn't.

I started crying then, crying so hard I couldn't see another thing.

My dad had to call my name three times before I heard him. "LeeAnn! LeeAnn! LeeAnn! You all right, hon?"

"I am," I called back. "But Smiley's not."

My dad didn't answer. He just said, "Hold on. We're coming."

Hearing my dad's voice made me cry all over again. It made me remember when my cat got run over by the tractor. My dad told me then that when a person dies and goes to heaven, well, all the dogs and cats she ever had will come running to meet her.

So I was comforting myself by thinking that

someday I'd see Smiley running to meet me, tail wagging, face living up to his name.

My dad and Fred, a man who worked on the farm, came out in the truck. They got ropes on Toro and led him away. He had got the meanness out of his system for the moment and went along quietly. Fred drove off with the bull, and I started climbing down.

My dad met me at the bottom of the tree. I looked over to where Smiley lay. "I gotta say good-bye."

"The dog's not dead, if that's what you're thinking."

"He's not?"

"No, he's got a hole in his shoulder and he's in shock, but I think he's going to be all right. Soon as Fred puts the bull up, we'll put Smiley in the truck and take him to the vet."

I went over to Smiley and knelt down and said what I hoped was the truth. "You're going to be all right."

And Smiley did get all right. You can still see the hole in his shoulder, where the fur didn't grow back. It's round and it reminds me of a medal.

So, if Smiley doesn't get this medal, I won't be too disappointed. He's already got the one that counts.

Bear

I remember it like it was yesterday. A car pulled up beside my daddy's truck at the stoplight. A little boy in the backseat rolled down his window and yelled, "Hey, there's a bear in the back of your truck."

I looked at our big Newfoundland, and it struck me. The boy was right. Our new dog looked exactly like a bear. I had been trying to think of a name ever since we got the dog. I've never been very good at that. Now I had my name.

Bear!

Bear is the smartest dog I have ever known. He sees something once and he can do it. The day we got Bear he watched me go out the back door. Next thing I knew he was putting his big paw on that handle and pushing it down. Now he can open our back door as well as any person. Bear watched my father go out for the newspaper. Now Bear goes out for the newspaper every morning, then he rings the doorbell to get back in.

As smart as Bear is, that's how dumb Snowball is. She's the big white fluffy dog that lives next door. Her biggest problem is that she's wild. She runs everywhere. If there's not enough room to run, Snowball sort of dances or prances around. She's never still, and her running always seems to lead to no good.

Last Fourth of July we were setting off fire-crackers, and Snowball grabbed one and took off. We tried to catch her, but she kept running like it was some kind of game. The firecracker blew up in her mouth, and she's still got the scar on her lip.

Once Snowball ran after the spot from Mr. Wilbanks's flashlight. When it got to the end of the room and started up the wall, Snowball didn't stop. She ran smack into the wall. She's still got a little bald spot on her head where she hit.

Anyway, on the day in question, it was Snowball's running that started it all. Bear and I were looking out the back window at the lake, watching the snow come down. I was wishing the lake was frozen through so I could go ice-skating. Bear was probably thinking the same thing. He loves the lake. In the summer he swims in it, and in the winter he chases me around and pulls me across the ice.

Suddenly Bear barked. I looked over at the Wilbankses' house and saw Snowball racing around the corner. They don't usually let Snowball out by herself. I guess it's because she runs so much. Anyway, Snowball flew down the hill and right out onto the ice.

I gasped. It was early December, way too early to think about going on the ice. Snowball's not a huge dog but certainly heavy enough to fall through.

I tried to open the window to yell, but it all happened too fast. Snowball was running at top speed. When she was about fifty yards out, she stopped. Her legs were spread in an unnatural way. She tilted her head to the side as if she was listening. She looked like those toy dogs whose heads rotate side to side. I gasped and Bear made a whining noise. We both knew what was going to happen next.

In an instant Snowball disappeared straight down into the icy water.

Bear and I stared at the spot of broken ice. It

seemed like an eternity, but finally Snowball bobbed back up. She immediately started clawing her way around the edge of the hole trying to get out. It was useless. Her paws slipped off the ice with every pull.

A terrible hopelessness swept over me. Last winter Daddy and I had watched a deer drown after falling through the ice. That deer had tried to claw his way out. I wanted to run out and help the deer, but Daddy said it was too dangerous. The deer finally gave up and disappeared beneath the ice.

This was much worse than the deer. I knew Snowball. She had lived next door to us for five years.

Bang!

The back door slammed shut. Bear was gone.

I didn't get my coat or anything. I just ran out after him.

"Come back," I yelled to Bear.

He ignored me. He went bounding down the hill.

I expected him to stop at the edge of the lake. Instead, he ran right out onto the ice.

"Bear. Nooooooooooo," I screamed. "The ice is too thin."

Bear kept running. He has always been surefooted

on the ice. I felt a spark of hope. Maybe Bear could somehow pull Snowball out without falling in himself. If anyone could do it, Bear could. Bear can do just about anything.

Snowball saw Bear coming and clawed even harder.

Bear was almost to the hole, but he was running way too fast. If he didn't slow down, he'd end up . . .

I watched with horror as Bear leaped into that icy water with Snowball.

I opened my mouth to yell, but nothing came out.

I started to cry. Bear was not going to save Snowball. He was going to die with her. They were both going to slip away into that death hole like the deer.

I couldn't believe Bear would make such a mistake! Bear never makes mistakes.

Bear turned and lifted a giant paw into the air. I felt sick. Bear was going to try to claw his way out like Snowball. I didn't want to watch but I couldn't take my eyes off him.

With the force of a wrecking ball Bear's right paw smashed down on the edge of the hole and broke away a large chunk of ice. Then his left paw lifted from the water and smashed away another chunk. His right paw smashed down again. Then his left. Right. Left. Right. Bear's paws began rotating around like a giant ice-crushing machine. A pathway was forming from the hole to the shore.

A small jolt of hope ran through me. Bear's plan might work if he had time. A person can only survive a short time in icy water. But this was a dog, a big Newfoundland, with a thick double coat.

"Go, Bear, go," I screamed.

I've often heard that encouragement can make the difference between life and death.

"Go, Bear, go," I yelled over and over.

Bear continued smashing away at the ice, lengthening the pathway to shore. Snowball swam behind him, her eyes big and round.

By the time they reached the shore Mrs. Wilbanks had arrived with blankets. We bundled up both dogs and got them inside. We rubbed them with warm towels. When we finished, Mrs. Wilbanks took the towel off Snowball. I expected Snowball to run wild around the sofa like I'd seen her do so many times before. She didn't.

Snowball walked, and I mean walked, not danced or pranced, right over to Bear and licked him in the face. Then Bear got excited and he ran around the sofa. It was the funniest thing I have ever seen. Snowball sat still while big old Bear ran around the sofa.

13

It's been six months since then. Snowball doesn't have a single scar to show for the accident. She's still wild, though. I guess some things never change, including Bear. He's still the smartest dog I have ever known. That's why Bear is my hero.

Munchkin

Don't like dogs. Never have. Pesky things.

Some of the big ones do some good, I suppose—herd sheep and rescue mountain climbers—but, I ask you, what's the good of those little dogs who just take up room on the sofa? Sofa pillows, that's what they are, but sofa pillows that won't stay put.

Dog next door was one of those four-legged sofa pillows. No good whatsoever. Pesky dog, name was Punchkin or Munchkin. I never could get it straight.

Dog would come in my garden like she owned it, like I planted the flowers for her to roll in.

"She loves your flowers," the woman next door would say—woman was pesky too. "We always know when Munchkin's been in your yard—she smells so sweet."

"Madam," I would reply, "I also know when Punchkin's been in my yard, because the flower beds have holes in them."

And the woman would laugh. Laugh! As if flower beds with holes in them like donuts were amusing!

Now, this year I was given a great honor. My garden was chosen to be in what they call the Parade of Roses. Judges go from home to home, judge the roses, and award prizes.

I was determined to win a blue ribbon. I deserved to win one; my roses, particularly my Lady Diana and my Lord George, were things of perfection.

Leading up to my rose garden were my flower beds, which, though they wouldn't be judged, must be perfection too. That was why it was so, so pesky to come out and see a round Punchkin-sized hole in the begonias.

The other morning I came out to work on my roses and there was Dunchkin sitting in the middle of the path. Pesky look on her face.

I said, "What is it now?" And I looked over and there were two weeds sticking up in my petunia patch. I bent down to pull out the weeds, and Munchkin rushed forward and grabbed my shirtsleeve.

"Now you've gone too far," I said to the dog.

I tried to shake my arm free, but the dog wouldn't let go.

Then I looked over at my petunias and saw I had something in there besides weeds. A copperhead snake was curled up watching me, flicking out its tongue.

Well, I got out of there quick, and took Punchkin with me. I had to—she still had her teeth in my shirt.

I got a hoe, but when I got back to the petunias, the snake had had the good sense to take itself out of there. Never saw the thing again.

So that's what Punchkin did. I did win a blue ribbon for my Lord George rose, and when I got it, I took it right next door and gave it to the lady.

"For Punchkin," I said.

"Munchkin," she said.

"Whatever."

I give the dog credit. Dog saved me from getting snakebit. Even a pesky dog can turn out to be a hero, and Punchkin's mine.

Thank you.

Old Dog

We called him Old Dog because even when we first got him, when he came wandering into the trailer park, he was old. He had a bad hip and couldn't see anymore. Sometimes he would bump into furniture if we left a chair out from the kitchen table.

Old Dog might not get around well, but can Old Dog sing! Whenever I practice my flute, he howls along with the music until everyone at Mr. Frankie's trailer park, where we live, complains. Ms. Robinson, my teacher, let me bring him to school one day and let him come to band to sing. His favorite song is "Stars and Stripes Forever," and when I play that high part at the end, he howls along.

His best game is hide-and-seek. He can't see but he can sure smell. My brother, Tommy, holds him, and I hide. I run through the trailer and jump behind my bedroom door or under the blankets of my bed.

Hiding under the covers, I hear him come, nails scraping on the linoleum, occasional barks of happy excitement. I hear him stop at the door to sniff around for me. Then he's by the bed and that big black nose is sniffing, sniffing, and—pounce—he's on me, digging in the covers like crazy, and I'm laughing.

Tricks are fun but that's not why I'm nominating him for the My Hero award. I'm nominating Old Dog because he saved my life. Not only did he save my life, he saved the lives of twenty-six people all in one night.

Old Dog is not only smart, he's the bravest dog in the world. There is only one thing that Old Dog is afraid of and that is thunder.

When he hears thunder there's only one place that he wants to be and that is under my bed. He lies there trembling while the storm passes over us, and sometimes I crawl under with him, put my arms around him, and listen to the thunder rumble.

Tornadoes come fast in Georgia. We have a radio to warn us and a siren that's supposed to go off in time to let us know. I don't know where we'd go though. Trailers don't have basements.

Anyway, the night the tornado hit us the radio wasn't even on and the siren never sounded. It came suddenly, surprising Mom and Tommy and me in our sleep. They say you hear a roaring train when a tornado comes. To me it was more like a huge airplane roaring over, like a sonic boom.

The trailer tipped up in slow motion and rolled over and over like a giant had picked it up and thrown it. Then it smacked down hard on the ground and split into a million pieces.

Then quiet.

I remember how quiet it was. How still. How dark. I didn't know where I was. All I knew was that I was covered with stuff and that my leg hurt more than it had ever hurt before. I didn't know where Tommy was, or Mom. I heard thunder, and I started crying, because I knew that Old Dog was somewhere and that he was scared and there was no bed for him to get under.

Then I heard him. I heard the scratch of his nails.

I would have yelled, but I didn't have the breath in me, so I gave a soft whistle and I heard Old Dog bark. The scraping got louder and I heard him bark again.

He kept digging and scratching and barking like crazy, and pretty soon Mr. Frankie was pulling boards off me. Soon I heard sniffing and that big black nose was poking me and I put my arms around Old Dog.

Old Dog left and I could hear him through the night, finding everyone one by one. First Mom, then Tommy, then the people in the other trailers. He'd find them and Mr. Frankie would uncover them. He didn't stop until twenty-six people were saved.

Our town had a parade for Old Dog. He rode on the back of Mr. Frankie's pickup and the band marched ahead. I rode with Old Dog, and when they played "Stars and Stripes Forever" I played the high part on my flute and Old Dog sang and sang. This time no one complained at all.

Buster

I love Buster. He is the bravest and most remarkable dog in the world. If you'd asked me a year ago, I would have told you I didn't like Buster. It's not that Buster's not cute. He's plenty cute. He's a big yellow Lab that lives next door. His eyes look up in a sad sort of way. So you're wondering why I didn't like such a cute dog? He ate my toe.

I was cutting the grass in my front yard. I'm supposed to wear tennis shoes, but I had on my sandals. My foot slipped under the edge of the mower, and the blade cut off the tip of my toe. I couldn't move. I always freeze like that when something terrible happens.

I was standing there staring at my toe when out of nowhere came a yellow streak. Buster! He flew across the yard, grabbed my toe, and ran. That is why I did not like Buster.

Last summer Buster did something to change that forever. It was a hot day and I was in my front yard pulling weeds. My baby sister, Mandy, was napping in her stroller beside me. When Mandy is in the yard, Buster keeps an eye on her stroller. Buster has always had a thing for babies. Every time a mother walks by pushing a baby stroller, Buster sits up and he doesn't take his eyes off that stroller until it is out of sight.

This day Buster was sitting on his porch watching Mandy and me. I had been pulling weeds for almost an hour and was getting tired. I decided to step inside and pour myself a glass of water.

First I checked on Mandy. She was still asleep. I debated whether to drag her stroller up the front steps and inside the house while I got my drink. I decided against it. I didn't want to wake her up and listen to her yell for Mama, who had run to the store.

I would only be inside a minute. Nothing could happen in that short time.

Buster had been sitting on his porch. Now he was standing. He watched me like he knew what I was going to do. He was giving me a look—like I shouldn't leave Mandy alone.

"You're not my mother," I said in an ugly voice.

Buster wagged his tail.

I put my hands on my hips. "Quit staring! I'm not mowing today. No more *toes* for you."

I yanked open the door. "Watch Mandy while I'm gone," I said.

I don't know why I said that. Buster didn't understand me. And even if he did, what was he going to do? He's overweight. And those skinny legs weren't going to carry him anywhere, except to grab defenseless toes.

Buster walked to the edge of the porch, like he understood me or something.

I went inside.

It's hard to know what happened next. The garbage man said he lost control, claimed his brakes didn't work right. All I know is that I heard screeching tires.

I ran to the window. The garbage truck was barreling down our street, completely out of control. It hit a parked car, then swerved toward a telephone

pole across the street. The truck grazed the telephone pole. The wheels jerked left, and the truck
headed straight for our yard.

I froze. I wanted to run out and grab Mandy, but
my legs wouldn't move. I stood there like a statue. A
sick feeling washed over me. The truck was seconds
away. Suddenly, out of the corner of my eye, I saw a
streak of yellow.

Buster.

He dashed across our yard, and jammed his large
head into Mandy's stroller. His skinny legs never
quit moving. His head hit the stroller and he pushed
it into the next yard. The garbage truck bumped
over the curb, barely missing Buster, and crashed
into our porch.

All of a sudden I could move. I gasped a breath of
air and ran outside. The garbage man jumped out of
his truck. He said something—I don't remember
what it was. I grabbed Mandy out of her stroller
and hugged her tight. She yawned. She had slept
through the whole thing.

I started crying. I don't cry much. I don't know
why I did then. I just know that I couldn't have
stopped even if I had wanted to.

In the middle of hugging Mandy, I felt hot breath
on my neck. Buster. I whirled around and grabbed

him too. I don't think I have ever hugged anyone harder. I hugged him and scratched him. I think I even kissed him.

Buster licked my face. His tail wagged.

At that moment, Mom pulled into the driveway. She got out of the car and stared at the truck. Then she dropped her groceries and ran for Mandy and me. It was Mom and Mandy and Buster and me, all rolling around on the ground hugging and kissing each other.

My dad went out that night and bought Buster a steak.

After they towed the garbage truck out of our yard, I had lots of yard work to do. Buster came over and sat beside me while I worked.

He comes over all the time now. I tell him what I'm doing. He listens. Mandy loves him too, even though she doesn't know he saved her life. I kept the newspaper article for her.

My toe used to remind me how much I didn't like Buster. Now it reminds me how close we are.

Buster risked his own life to save Mandy. He is my hero . . . and Mandy's hero . . . and our whole family's hero.

Blue

"Speak, Blue, speak!" I bet I said that a thousand times when I first got the dog. But Blue would not bark.

He never barked. I mean, never.

If Blue wanted a thing, he'd find some other way to let you know.

Like, if he wanted to come inside the house, he would scratch at the door. There were scratch marks in the wood, but I never cared. Looked to me like it's a compliment to a house that the dog wants to come in and be with everybody.

Blue got his name because his mom was a

full-blooded blue tick hound. We never figured out who the father was, but Blue had the look of his mom.

Anyway, to get to the story, that morning—this was September, a Friday—I went into the woods. I took two things with me—my dog and my chain saw.

What I was going to do was cut down some tree branches that Mama said were cutting off her view of the lake.

I spent about two hours sawing a limb here, a limb there. I was standing at the edge of the lake, squinting up at the house—it was way up on the hill—and I decided there was just one more tree in the way of Mama's view of the lake.

I whistled for Blue to let him know I was about ready to head for home. I never knew exactly where Blue was in the woods, because he didn't bay or bark the way most hounds do. I figured he got his silence from his daddy.

Anyway, in about two minutes Blue showed up. He had dirt on his nose and I figured he'd been digging.

I walked up the hill a little ways to the offending tree. I cranked up my chain saw, raised it, whacked the limb.

I had in mind letting the chain saw swing down

away from my leg. I'd done it a hundred times like that. But I don't know what went wrong this time—maybe I was tired. Anyway, it happened so fast I was helpless. The saw came down right on my leg and cut all the way into the bone.

I dropped to the ground. Blood was pumping out of my leg. I never saw so much blood. I must have cut an artery. I grabbed my leg and held it tight, and the blood stopped pumping full-tilt, but blood was still squeezing out between my fingers, and when I let go of the leg the least little bit to get a better hold, blood pumped some more.

I don't mind admitting I was scared. I was over half a mile from home. I could call for help, but I had screamed when the chain saw hit me and Mama hadn't heard that. I could start crawling, but that looked like a long half-mile, and it was all uphill, and not flat land either—boulders and gullies, and me having to use both hands to stop the bleeding.

Well, I looked up and there was Blue. I said, "Blue, get Mama."

He looked at me like he didn't understand. I said it again. "Blue, get Mama."

He went a few steps up the hill, but he didn't look happy about it. The dog knew I was in trouble and he didn't want to leave.

I said it again, hard this time. "Blue, get Mama!"

He turned and started for the house. He never looked back, and I lost sight of him in the trees.

I waited. I didn't have a lot of hope, because, the way I figured it, Blue would go to the door, scratch, be let in, and that would be the end of it. Mama wouldn't think anything was wrong.

As I lay there, I felt myself getting weaker. I felt like I was about to faint, and I knew if I fainted that would be the end of me.

And then, as I lay there—dying, I thought—I heard something I never thought to hear in my life-time: Blue barking. It sounded far, far away—up at the house—and it was the sweetest sound I ever heard in my life.

When Mama heard Blue barking, she went straight to the phone and called 911. She said, "I don't know exactly what the trouble is, but my husband went out with the chain saw and only the dog came back and he's barking his head off."

The rescue squad came—got there in less than ten minutes—and Blue showed them the way to where I lay. They tied up my leg and carried me up the hill on a stretcher.

So the way I figure it is this: If a hero is somebody that saves a person's life, then Blue is a hero.

Thinking back on it, I'm glad he wasn't a barker. I'm glad he saved his barking for when it was really needed. I wouldn't be standing here today if he hadn't.

Thank you.

Little Bit

It's a miracle that I'm able to be here tonight. I'll be ninety-three years old tomorrow and my knees are tight with arthritis. It hurts to sit in this wheelchair but I'll do it for the one who saved my life. It's all because of one cold wet nose, a trembling paw, a little ball of fur named Little Bit.

I came to Heavenly Manor in an ambulance. My home was taken away from me. "Too old" is what my daughter said. "Too old" is what everyone said. Every time someone said "too old" I gave up a little bit. I stopped crocheting the baby blankets that I sold at the Mountain Craft Store. I stopped taking care of my azaleas out in the backyard. And finally I just stopped.

"There's plenty to do here at Heavenly Manor," the nurse Jane would say. But all I did was watch TV. I tried to remember my house, my backyard with the azaleas, but slowly the memories began to fade.

"You need to eat, Miss Ophelia." "It's a pretty day outside." "You need to drink some water now." But I didn't want to eat or drink or look at the pretty day outside.

I don't know how long I sat, probably close to two months. Someone fed me and wheeled me in front of the TV, but there seemed to be nothing to live for.

One Wednesday, as I sat and looked at *The Price Is Right*, I felt something cold on my hand, cold and wet. I didn't look. "Go on," I said. "Go on like everyone else." I pulled back my hand, but all week I kept thinking of the memory of that cold wet nose and I realized that cold nose was the first time anyone or anything had touched me in a long time.

The next Wednesday they wheeled me out to the Happy Room again, and I sat watching *The Price Is Right*, and I felt it again, that cold wet nose pushing on my hand. "Shoo, you," I said. "I don't have anything for you."

The nose didn't leave, and this time I could feel the breath blowing on my hand.

The next Wednesday I wheeled myself out early and sat close to the door. When *The Price Is Right* came on I watched the door. *Wheel of Fortune* started. The dog wasn't coming, I thought, and just when I had decided to give up I felt it again—a cold wet nose. This time I didn't move my hand, and felt the coldness and wetness of the nose. Then the nose pushed under my hand and I felt a soft furry head.

Warmth on my hand—breath and life. All of a sudden I remembered how I had felt in my backyard digging in the dirt, planting my flowers.

The next day I got dressed.

I look forward to Wednesdays now, when Little Bit comes to visit. The girl from the Pet Mobile is friendly and reminds me of my youngest grandchild, Sarah.

When Jane saw the sweater that I had crocheted for Little Bit she asked me to make one for her dog, Pokey. I think I'm back in business.

Every Wednesday, Little Bit heads for me first. She's a small dog, soft brown hair, sleek and shiny, with one white paw. Cold wet nose, soft brown head. Warm body.

Some of the dogs that they bring do tricks or run

around from person to person, but Little Bit just sits. She rests her head on my lap and looks up at me with big brown eyes.

I think she needs a warmer sweater for winter. Blue would be pretty with her brown fur. I'll ride the shuttle bus to the mall tomorrow to buy some yarn.

I read one time in a book about survival in the arctic wilderness, the rule of three: You can go three minutes without air. You can go three hours without shelter. You can go three days without water. Three weeks without food. Three months without love.

Little Bit may not have saved me with food or shelter, but sure as I live and breathe Little Bit saved me with love.

She's my hero.

Dopey

There were seven pups. They'd been named Grumpy, Happy, Sneezy, Dopey, Doc, Bashful, and Sleepy, after the seven dwarfs. And, wouldn't you know it, the only one that hadn't been sold was Dopey.

We brought Dopey home and named him Harvey, but we couldn't quit calling him Dopey, because that's what he was.

The dog would bark at anything that was out of place. If I dropped a book on the living-room floor, Dopey would bark at it. To shut him up, I'd have to say, "Dopey, it's just a book," and take it over there and show him.

Here are just a few of the things I said to Dopey: "Dopey, it's just a bedroom slipper." "Dopey, it's just a paper bag." One time out in the yard I even had to say, "Dopey, it's just a leaf."

We kept hoping he'd grow out of it, but so far he hadn't.

On the day this story happened, Dopey and I were in the backseat of the car. My mom pulled into the parking lot of a strip mall and went in Hair Today to get a haircut. She said she would only be about fifteen minutes, but I'd brought a book along. Dopey and I sat out in the car.

I was reading, and Dopey was looking for something suspicious to bark at.

It was hot, but we had the windows rolled down, and there was a breeze.

We'd been there about five minutes when Dopey stuck his head out the window and started barking.

I looked. I said, "It's just a car, Dopey."

Dopey kept barking.

"It is just a car!"

Dopey kept barking.

"Oh, all right."

I picked Dopey up—he fit nicely right under my arm—and carried him over to the car.

"See, it's just a—"

And I never got to finish the sentence.

On the backseat of that car was a baby. In all this heat—there was a baby, and it looked like it was dead.

I knocked on the window to get its attention. It didn't move.

I tried to open the door.

It was locked.

I ran around to the other door.

It was locked.

I ran in Hair Today.

I yelled, "There's a baby on the backseat of a car and I think it's dead."

Well, Hair Today emptied so fast, it was like those cattle stampedes you see on TV. I had to jump out of the way to keep from getting trampled.

My mom led the way to the car—she figured out which one it was because it was the only one close to ours.

"Somebody get me a brick," one lady yelled, rattling the doors and running around the car.

One lady ran back in Hair Today to call 911, but my mom wasn't going to wait for any rescue squad or any brick.

My mom threw open the trunk of our car, grabbed

the tire iron, ran to the front window, pulled back like she was getting ready to hit a home run, and knocked out the window.

Well, the baby was not dead, but the man from 911 said that if my mom hadn't acted when she did the baby would have been. "Another two or three minutes in that heat would have done it."

We waited until the mom came out, and you wouldn't believe what she'd been doing all this time. She'd been playing video poker! She said she'd just meant to play one game, but she got so wrapped up in it, she forgot all about the baby.

My mother gave her a long talking to about taking better care of her baby.

"Why, if my dog hadn't barked and if my son hadn't gone to see what the trouble was, you wouldn't even have a baby!"

So that was how Dopey became a hero. Some people might think Dopey was just barking for the pleasure of it, but I don't believe that. I believe Dopey knew there was a baby in that car and the baby was in real trouble.

If Dopey does become Hero, if he does get a

medal, and I put it beside his bed, he'll probably bark at it, and I'll say, "Dopey, it's just a medal."

Wait a minute! Just a medal! What am I saying? "Dopey, it's the My Hero medal!" That's what I'll say. That's what I hope I get to say.

The Daily Chronicle

My Hero Chosen

FRIDAY EVENING the eight finalists in the My Hero contest appeared before the three-judge panel, as well as a noisy packed house. After much deliberation the judges chose a winner and issued this statement:

We love all these dogs. Each one possesses a unique gift that makes him or her a hero. We would therefore like to issue the following awards:

The David and Goliath Award—to Smiley, who fought a giant of a bull.

The Feet of Strength Award—to Bear, whose magnificent paws saved a friend.

The Sharp Eye Award—to Munchkin, who knew a snake when he saw one.

The Good Neighbor Award—to Buster, who laid down his life for the baby next door.

The Bark of the Year Award—to Blue, who saved his bark for when it was needed.

The Kindest Heart Award—to Little Bit, whose love brought a renewed love of life.

The IQ Award—to Dopey, who used his good sense to save a life.

MY HERO AWARD

Because of the many lives he saved and because it was necessary for him to overcome physical difficulties to perform his act of heroism, we award the My Hero medal to Old Dog.